THE VIRUS IN THE AIR

MONA YADAV

To my sister Komal,
Thank you for your unwavering support, enthusiasm, and belief in me. You encouraged me to keep going, and you always reminded me why I needed to finish this—not just because you wanted to read it, but above all, because you wanted to see me as a published author. You've been my biggest cheerleader, urging me to publish, to finish, and to share this story with the world. This book is as much yours as it is mine. Thank you for being there every step of the way.

Love you, always!

Contents

CHAPTER ONE

BELLA AND HER CHILDREN

"Don't look up, okay?" said Bella. "Keep your eyes on the ground. No matter what happens—or what voices you hear—you must not look or go in that direction, or any direction they come from."

Both kids looked at their mommy and nodded.

"Do you both get that?" Bella cried, her voice rising with desperation as she thumped the seat. Her fingers trembled, twisting and untwisting the fabric of her dress in restless panic. She was so overwhelmed by fear and the weight of responsibility that she didn't even notice her children's eyes welling up with tears—or how their small hands clutched each other in silent fright.

All she could focus on was keeping them safe, even if it meant frightening them in the process.

"Say it out loud!" she demanded, her tone harsher than she intended.

"Mommy!" Both kids cried, their eyes brimming with tears as they nodded. They knew something was wrong outside, but seeing their mother upset and yelling at them for the first time made it even worse, even though they had been following her instructions all along.

Bella didn't want to take any risks that could endanger her children. This wasn't just the biggest battle of her life—to find a safe place—it was also her greatest responsibility.

"It's okay... we... we'll be alright. Just... just follow me, and we'll be safe," Bella whispered, her voice trembling as she squeezed her children's hands tightly.

She pulled her children close and hugged them, feeling the rapid beat of her daughter's heart sync with her own. Bella knew exactly what she had to do the moment they got out of the car: find safety—no matter what it took.

The windows and windshield were covered, making the task even harder. Once they stepped outside, they would have to navigate blindly.

"Are you both ready?" asked Bella calmly.

They both nodded, their hands clenched tightly in their laps.

"Don't worry, kids. We're safe in these suits—as long as you don't look up and keep your heads down, okay?" Bella said.

"Okay. On the count of three, I'll open the car door, and we'll rush to any building that looks safe. Don't worry," she added in a hurried voice.

"Okay. One... two... three—go!"

They set foot on the ground. The city was no longer a city—it was a cemetery. It felt more like a place of the dead. Time had stopped, as if it had refused to move forward. No birds, no people—and it felt as if even God had lost the battle against the demon. The silence was deafening, and the scent of death hung thick in the air.

Bella moved quickly between the bodies, taking long strides. Her hands were tightly interlocked with her children's soft, tiny fingers. She wasn't sure if she would find the others or the building, but she was certain there was one shelter left—where the last remaining people on Earth were staying.

In her last conversation with her friend Arthur, a scientist like herself, he had told her about a large, secure building where they were taking refuge—just before all communication had been cut off.

Her mind was overwhelmed—too consumed by thoughts, the stench seeping through her suit, and the constant overthinking. It was all starting to boggle her mind. The farther she moved from the car, the more her anxiety grew. She could no longer feel her body moving—it was as if only her legs were pushing her forward, taking her toward safety. Every breath she took felt like a step closer to death, and strangely, it brought a sense of relief.

"Mom!" cried the boy. "Where's Girl?"

Bella looked around, astonished, her heart pounding in her chest like a drumbeat. She clenched her dress in her fist, and just then, she saw a building as Arthur described it at some distance.

"Boy, you go ahead to that building and ask for help. If you feel someone inside, just say my name—they know me—and make them open the door. Understood? Go!"

The boy rushed toward the building as instructed, and Bella moved to find her daughter, Girl. She scanned the bodies around her, her mind struggling to process and differentiate, to recognise her daughter.

Finally, she spotted a thick white suit and a helmet on top. Bella quickly ran toward it.

"Girl!" she cried. "Come on, baby, let's go!"

But Girl wasn't conscious—she had fainted, Bella guessed. Without hesitation, Bella scooped her up and rushed toward the building.

Bella's heart sank as she saw her son still outside the building, crying.

"Open the door!" Bella yelled. "Dr. Arthur, it's me, Bella. Can you hear me? Please, open the door! I'm with my kids—they're so small and scared, too. I know... I know you're scared, but please believe me. I'm alright, and the kids are too. I'm not lying. Dr. Arthur, can you hear me?"

Bella cried out, her voice breaking. "Everything is in vain," she mumbled, her head slumping against the door. Her body weakened, and she could no longer stand—she collapsed, her body sinking to the ground in front of the door.

Then, suddenly, she fell inside. An old woman grabbed the boy's hand and pulled him inside, slamming the door shut behind them.

CHAPTER TWO

INSIDE THE BUILDING

"Are you alright, baby?" Bella asked her daughter.

"Come here," she said to her son, pulling both of them into a tight hug and kissing them on their foreheads.

"Thank you so much, guys! Thanks," Bella said, elated.

A few people stood around them, watching quietly. Bella felt a wave of relief—her children were safe and with her.

But now, she needed to find her friend, Arthur. At that moment, she saw him, standing right in front of her.

"Bella! Is that you?" he said, his face lighting up with delight. "Are you alright?"

"Hi!," Bella said with a delighted face. "I'm finally here with you all, it is all good now."

"Come with me. I have something to show you."

Bella followed Arthur. She saw many people in different rooms—some playing with their kids, others feeding them, teaching, and making funny sounds and gestures with newborn babies. Everyone seemed happy, as if nothing happened, or perhaps pretending to. Every corner of the building smelled sweet and fresh.

After walking for a while, they reached a room that was empty except for a few chairs, a desk, two beautiful black-and-white paintings on the walls, and a small red umbrella hanging on the far side, with the word 'Alien' written on it.

"Feels like home again," Bella said, looking around. "It's been a very long time for us."

"So, how did you get here?" Arthur asked.

"Underground."

"Underground?"

"It was an old storeroom, deep underground. My husband bought the house before he went to Idaho. I didn't find out about it until later, but he had bought it knowing it had a storeroom underground. I think he knew what was coming," Bella explained, her voice tinged with sadness. "But he never told me. Instead, he kept telling me to stay below ground for a while... and that 'while' turned into two months."

"And did you make it here by car?"

"What else could I have done?" Bella sighed. "We ran out of food, and since the last call with you, the network's been down."

Bella gazed around the room, her eyes scanning everything, as she had nothing more to say. Then, her gaze landed on something. "What's that umbrella, and why is it tagged with the name Alien?"

"That's what I wanted to show you. We found it near a boy named Harley."

"But it doesn't make sense that you kept it. I mean, it's just an ordinary umbrella, right? Why hang it there like it's precious? Just an umbrella, huh?"

"I know. But, would you let me speak?" he said walking toward the wall as Bella followed him. "Harley wasn't just any ordinary boy."

Arthur took a deep breath and started: so, basically, Harley's DNA was unlike anything we've ever encountered in our lives. It took us a few days to uncover the secrets, but we finally did it. And if you were here, you would've seen with your own eyes how strange he looked—his large head, and his eyes, which were like those of a drunkard.

"Was he alive when you found him?" Bella asked, showing no interest in his appearance.

"His condition was bad, but he survived for a while," Arthur said, settling comfortably into the chair. "Harley possessed a rare genetic mutation—one never observed before. This mutation granted him an extraordinary ability: the power to see glimpses of the future."

"That sounds absurd! It's impossible!" Bella cried in astonishment.

"Well, isn't it true that every impossibility has a beginning? This could be the one, and eventually, it might not sound so impossible."

"Well said. Well said," Bella laughed out loud.

Bella noticed two doctors approaching them, smiling at Arthur. They were walking briskly, as if there were an emergency. One was a tall, thin young woman with blonde hair, her pretty smile lighting up her face. The other was a tall, handsome young man with bowl-cut hair and a broad smile.

"Sir, did you call us?" the young woman asked gently. "Is everything okay?"

"Yes, everything's fine," Arthur replied. "Bella just needs a health checkup."

"No! I don't need one, Arthur. I'm fine!" Bella immediately responded, looking at him with a furrowed brow. "What?"

"You're not fine. You need it."

"Arthur, I'm a scientist. Don't forget that. If I'm not well, I'll see the doctors myself," Bella said, her voice tinged with irritation.

"But what's the problem, Bella?" Arthur asked. "It'll only take a few minutes."

"The problem is, we don't have time," Bella argued, glancing at her children. She lowered her voice. "And I have kids. I can't let anything happen to them."

"This is an argument now," said Arthur.

"No, it's not!"

"Okay! So, can you tell us a little about conditions outside? I mean, how does the air smell?"

"It was awful—like burned tires or something that could—" Bella suddenly stopped as she heard herself speaking. She looked at their faces and saw the expressions she expected. The doctors stared at her, offering sheepish smiles, while Arthur walked over to the kids and whispered something to them, making them smile.

"Okay!" Bella sighed. "I'm going."

"Dr. Neviah and Dr. Caller, please take the kids too," Arthur instructed.

They all entered a room where most things were covered with white sheets. The uncovered items included a few large machines, a refrigerator, and some ragged couches. Despite its disarray, the room had its own charm—it felt like a perfect place to live. However, it was also clear to Bella that this room was not meant to be accessed by anyone, a fact she deduced from the way it was arranged.

Dr. Caller checked on Bella while the kids were with Dr. Neviah at a distance in the room.

"So, how long have you been working here, Dr. Caller?" Bella asked.

"Not too long—just over a month, I think," Dr. Caller smiled.

"Is he your boyfriend?" Bella asked suddenly.

Caller looked at her and grinned. "Er... Could you please give me your left hand? I need to administer an injection into your arm." She talked very professionally.

Bella smiled and extended her left hand. There was a moment of silence between them as Caller injected the needle, while the kids giggled from a distance.

"Done!" Caller smiled.

"So, have you found any way to connect to Mars for help?" Bella asked curiously.

"Yes, we've tried many times, but no help yet."

"There must be some issue with the system or the connection," Bella replied. "Are you suggesting that they don't want to help us?"

"Can't say, maybe."

"No, that can't happen."

"Why are you so sure?"

"Because Arthur isn't just a scientist and a good doctor—he's also a skilled mathematician and astrophysicist," Bella replied quickly, her words rushing out.

"But they now have machines with better algorithms and more advanced AI," replied Caller. "Machines that are more powerful, intelligent, and faster than humans."

"Yes, they do," Bella acknowledged, rising from the chair. "But that's not how things work. If we created them, we would be cleverer and sharper."

"That's true," Caller agreed. "But Arthur isn't the only one. There are others up there, maybe better than any of us. I respect Arthur, but... he is old now..."

"No! They need Arthur. He might be old, but his mind still holds the power to save us all. We all know what he has done for us. People are up there on Mars, happy and safe. The Earth is calling for our death, but we're still here, still fighting to make our way off this planet. And it's all because of Arthur," Bella said, bitterness lacing her voice as she tried to calm herself with the same words.

Caller stood still, looking uneasy. Bella felt the tension and decided not to make things any more awkward than they already were. Without saying another word, she turned and left the room.

As she walked back to Arthur, Bella felt a weight in her chest. She knew she had spoken harshly, and it didn't feel right. She shouldn't have let her frustration get the best of her.

Arthur was sitting in his usual spot, a chair near the desk, absorbed in a book. He had brown eyes, always hidden beneath a brown cowboy hat. A healthy, white man in his sixties, Arthur had a habit of carrying small vials of medicine in his pockets, which he'd take periodically throughout the day.

"Hi, Arthur," said Bella.

"Bella! Come in," Dr. Arthur replied with a delighted voice.

"Can you tell me why the air didn't affect people inside the building when we came in, or when they opened the door?"

"Did it affect you?" Arthur asked.

"Well, I wouldn't say yes," Bella smiled.

"Yeah, I think the air isn't that dangerous—at least not here, not yet," Arthur said, setting the book aside and resting his hands on the desk. "Also, the smell... that sweet fragrance that feels like home, helps neutralise any harmful elements in the air, making it less of a threat."

"But I'm sure this sweet fragrance can't kill the viruses in the air," Bella said thoughtfully. "This air has killed thousands of people outside."

"No! I—I just told you," Arthur said, shaking his head. "It's not the air, as far as I know. It's the whisper that manipulates people and makes them do what it tells them."

"But in Idaho, my husband died because of the virus in the air," Bella responded.

"I thought it was a heart attack," Arthur said, confused.

"No, it was the virus," Bella insisted.

"Bella, it's possible that the virus is spreading. In Idaho, yes, the virus was the cause of death, but here in California, it's not affecting people in the same way, not yet. Here, it's the whisper."

"And what exactly is this whisper?" Bella asked, her brow furrowed in concern.

"Maybe the whisper comes before the virus, setting up a polluted environment," Arthur speculated. "There have been thousands of cases where people have stabbed themselves or even resorted to cannibalism, like something out of a zombie story. And, like you said, the smell—burnt plastic, something worse—creates the perfect conditions for the virus to thrive."

"That sounds like..." Bella hesitated, her eyes widening with the realisation.

"Not pleasant?" Arthur finished for her.

"Yeah," Bella laughed nervously. "It's like a ghostly dance, making weird noises before it strikes."

"I can't believe it, Bella," Arthur chuckled, shaking his head. "Seriously?"

Before Bella could say anything else, she heard the familiar sound of her children approaching. They stood at the doorway, waiting patiently for their mother to notice them. Bella quickly walked over to them, kissed each of them on the forehead, and held their hands tightly. With a warm smile, she turned to Arthur, who smiled back before getting up and walking toward them.

"Let me show you to your room," Arthur said kindly, leading the way out of the room. "It's on the second floor."

The room was small but charming, one of the few on the second floor with a glass ceiling. Through it, they could see the sky, now a dull grey with no clouds in sight. The space was modest, with a few single sofas scattered around and a large study table tucked into one corner. Colourful mats were laid across the floor, adding a touch of warmth. Like most rooms in the building, this one was painted white, with plain walls—no pictures or frames to decorate the space. Yet, it was the smell that filled the room, a sweet, comforting fragrance that made it feel oddly homey.

"Thanks, Arthur, for doing all of this," Bella said with a grateful smile.

"No problem! I've already had your food brought up to the room. It should be on the table. I think it's getting late now. You should get some good rest, and we'll work tomorrow, alright?"

"Yeah, definitely. Have a good night," Bella wished and settled into the room.

After they ate the food, they lay down on the floor, too drained to do anything else.

"Sky's beautiful at night," said the girl, her voice soft as she lay beside her mother.

"Yes, it is," Bella answered, looking up through the glass ceiling, her thoughts wandering.

"How big is the sky, mommy?"

Bella paused for a moment, thinking before she replied, "It's unpredictable, sweetie."

"So, what is predictable, mommy?"

"The universe is unpredictable, and that's the only thing that's predictable," Bella said thoughtfully, as if explaining it to a teenager. The girl smiled and giggled. Though only five years old, she loved engaging in deep conversations with her mom. She was wearing a black hoodie, short jean pants, and had short, curly hair—her big, adorable eyes shining in the dim light.

The girl turned her gaze to the sky, busy counting the stars. Meanwhile, the boy stayed quiet, lost in his own thoughts.

"What's wrong, Boy?" Bella asked, glancing to her left.

"What is our name?" he asked slowly, carefully choosing his words.

"Hmmm... so who told you that 'Boy' isn't a name?" Bella asked curiously.

"Dr. Neviah. He asked our names. We told him, but he laughed and said it wasn't a name."

"Hmmm, the tall, thin one?" Bella turned her head toward her son.

"He was very nice and gave us chocolates," he added, his voice soft.

"Good!" Bella smiled, kissed his forehead, and tucked him in. "Now, it's time to sleep. It's getting late, alright?"

She looked to her right, and her baby girl was already fast asleep, her little form curled up peacefully beside her.

Days passed in a quiet, uneasy rhythm. Everything remained the same—except the air. Its colour had begun to shift, turning increasingly grey and smoky, thickening like a warning. Day by day, it grew worse. Men and women grew anxious.

Children, once lively and playful, spent more time gazing out through the glass roof than playing on the floor.

During these days, Bella and Arthur worked tirelessly. Together, they made some progress with the machines, attempting to establish a connection with the people on Mars. It was their only hope. Arthur explained the plan to others, making it sound possible, almost simple. But it wasn't. Deep down, he knew how complicated it truly was.

Still, he did it for their peace of mind. He wanted to give them something to believe in, something to hold on to. And for a while, it worked. But Arthur had always known that time was their enemy. If something else went wrong before the machine could be ready, everything would collapse.

And then, the day he feared... finally arrived.

One morning, when Arthur was strolling alone in the basement, someone came rushing down to call him upstairs with an urgency in his voice. As Arthur stepped onto the ground floor, he saw everyone gathered and waiting for him. Caller was prepared for something to say. The moment she saw him, she began speaking without hesitation, as if she had prepared her words long before he arrived.

"Dr. Arthur, I've got some bad and good news," she said at once. "Which one should I tell first?"

"Does it matter?" Arthur muttered. "The bad one first, please."

"We're running out of food."

"How long do we have?"

"Less than a week."

"I was hoping for at least a month." Arthur took off his hat and sank into the chair that was placed for him. "All right, what's the good news, Dr. Caller?"

"We found a grocery store nearby."

Arthur raised a brow. "A grocery store?"

"It's five kilometers from here."

"Five kilometers?" Arthur let out a dry laugh. "And how exactly do you think we'll get there?"

There was a moment of silence. Caller stared blankly at Bella, waiting for her to respond.

"We have a car, Arthur, in the basement," said Bella finally, hesitantly. "I know the windshield is broken, but—"

"I know that there is a car in the basement. And yes, you're right— the windshield is broken. Of course I know all of this," interrupted Arthur in a hurried and distressed voice. He pulled out his handkerchief and wiped his forehead. "But what about that?"

At that moment, Bella lost faith in her plan. She could see where it was headed and knew for certain Arthur would reject the idea, and maybe he'd be right. But not continuing with what she was saying felt even worse.

"This is Cassandra," Bella continued. "I met her last night. She's skilled with repairs. I think she can help us reach the store safely," Bella finished.

"Go on," Arthur said, half-amused.

"I can fix the glass," Cassandra said, meeting Arthur's eyes calmly. "I've done it many times. And I have the tools with me."

At the moment when Cassandra was speaking, Arthur was thinking, How dumb can someone be? Dumber than this? Of course, we know, lady, that you are the one who promises to fix the glass—why else would you be introduced? And how? How exactly does someone fix a broken windshield without replacing it with glass? With some kind of paper? Or tape? Or what?

"That's great," Caller said when Cassandra finished speaking.

"What's so great about it, Dr. Caller?" Arthur snapped, his voice rising as he looked around, exasperated. "Bella, what's going on here?"

Bella walked to him as he took out his medicine from his shirt's pocket and asked Neviah for some water.

"We have a week's worth of food left," she said gently. "Cassandra has an idea. Why not give it a chance? We might find something useful—maybe even sealed food."

"What food, Bella?" said Arthur with an efforted, gentle voice. "Everything out there is destroyed—no food, no clean water, not even air. We're manufacturing what little we have here. Risking lives for a ruined store is a foolish idea. We should be focusing on connecting to Mars. That's our only real hope. And now we're on a deadline... I hope we're clear on it"

"But there's a chance—"

"A chance?" Arthur interrupted. "It's not just the air. It's the whisper. It will kill you, tear you apart, and you know that."

He took the bottle of water from Neviah and swallowed his medicine.

The room went quiet. One by one, the others returned to their work, disappointed and unsure. Only Bella stayed behind with Arthur, asking gently if he was feeling alright. They spoke for a while—about life, memories, and moments lost—until Arthur's breathing steadied again. Then, as always, they returned to work, side by side, until the sun began to sink.

CHAPTER THREE

BENEATH THE GROUND

Everyone was mentally shattered when they realised that death was certain, and began to truly believe it after hearing the words from Arthur himself, the very man they had placed their faith in, the one they had built all their hopes around. They knew then that death would come—if not tomorrow, then the day after.

That day at night, everyone gathered at the table to eat together, trying to hold on to hope and give each other strength. The situation was critical. Unfortunately, neither Bella nor Arthur had joined the table. Discussion started at the table on how to survive themselves instead of relying on anyone anymore, especially not Arthur.

Some suggested that they kill themselves so their child could live. Others, colder and brutal, proposed killing the children, claiming they wouldn't survive on their own anyway.

Cassandra suggested digging the ground and making a hole, knowing that there was no idea as awful as the one she was proposing. She still chose to propose it for some reason. She proposed her idea first to two middle-aged men who were tall and big in size. One of them was horrible looking: he was bald and had a cut on his neck, and his teeth were unevenly distributed. When Cassandra put her idea to everyone, many disagreed, but some agreed and argued that the idea was not that bad and must be kept as part of the plan.

A heated argument broke out, each person clinging to their own version of survival, and none was listening to the other but raising their voices louder than the next person. Someone slammed a chair against the wall. Another shouted, "We're going to die anyway! We should at least try something!" A woman sobbed in frustration as her husband pulled her away from the crowd.

In a corner stood Caller, silently observing the chaos unfold. Her eyes drifted across the room—from the men who were trying to outshout one another, to the anxious mothers clutching their children, and finally to the children themselves, their faces pale with fear and confusion. Caller almost laughed—not out of joy, but disbelief—as she glanced at the main door and remembered the desolation that lay beyond it. The world outside was a graveyard of silence, smoke, and deathly whispers.

But reason had long abandoned the room.

Later that night, when Caller was gone to Neviah to sleep, four foolish people—driven more by desperation than courage—decided to carry out Cassandra's idea at the first hour of sunrise. These four people were: a middle-aged man with the body of a hulk; another man, tall as a pillar, bald with an unsettlingly ugly face, and a long cut running down his neck. The third was Cassandra's young and beautiful friend. And the fourth—Cassandra herself—stood among them, calm but consumed by something deeper: malicious intent.

They planned to do it when the clock struck 4 O'clock. They didn't think twice about what they would do after digging a hole or even after reaching the grocery store. They had no idea of what or if there were possibilities of digging for 5km. All they knew was this: they had to do something. And digging felt like doing something.

As the hours passed, whispers spread like smoke, and people started murmuring the details of the plan with trembling lips, and each time it passed from one person to the next, it sounded more dreadful. They said it was a heinous act that was about to take place in the morning, and it sounded horrible to each and every mind, knowing that it was one of the things Arthur strictly forbade even trying. A young boy had even informed Arthur and Bella about the plan while everyone was still gathered at the table. When he returned, he told the others that both Arthur and Bella had strictly opposed the idea, calling it a pointless effort that would lead nowhere. But the boy was quickly dismissed and cast out from the crowd.

And now, the forbidden was only hours away.

Early the next morning, Cassandra, along with her friend and two tall bodybuilders, reached the basement—followed by the rest of the crowd. Caller was still asleep in a room with Neviah.

Without wasting a minute, the two bodybuilders began digging. They both were healthy and strong, yet they kept hitting and hitting, but very little was done after keeping for an hour. When they finally broke through the hard surface, they held their shovel up in the air and hit it hard into the soil. The shovels finally hit a thrip—the size of a turtle in the dead soil—piercing straight through its body and into the soil that smelled like rotten eggs.

The two men, who had been digging with passion and desperation, felt instant regret. They shook the shovel and pulled it free from the thrip's corpse. The sight of their shovel covered with a black, thick, and sticky substance disgusted them. Both stumbled two inches back and puked on their own feet. The soil was black ash—lightweight and hollow— infested with thrips and scarab beetles savagely devouring one another. It looked as if the soil itself was calling for death. The brutal death of humanity.

The crowd went wild. People stepped back, bumping into one another in panic. Cassandra and her friend were among them, while those two big and bulky men just stood there, frozen in disbelief at what their eyeballs were witnessing.

Everyone stared, motionless and dazed, like fools. Just a few moments later, scarab beetles and thrips began crawling out of the soil—and just then, someone's mind clicked. A young boy, entangled in fear, shouted in a loud, cracking voice, "Pave the stone... stone back in the soil! Kill that beetle... there... there!" He pointed frantically. "It's coming out! Quick!" he screamed, his voice tearing from his throat as he danced around and ran back into the crowd.

The two men snapped back to their senses. They bent down, locked their fingers around heavy stones, and hurled them into the hole. Quickly, they paved over it with the cement that was there in the basement.

It went nothing like they had expected, and everyone was shocked by the horrifying scene—everyone except Cassandra. Her reaction was unsettlingly calm, as if she had known the consequences of the act all along.

Things had clearly gone wrong, and together they chose to keep it a secret once again from both Arthur and Bella. Neither Arthur nor Bella had time to wander or investigate—both were too busy working, trying to get as much done as possible. And in doing so, the hope of saving everyone had once again been rekindled in them.

As usual, the sun rose in the east, and people were doing their mundane activities— walking, eating, playing and making weird noises around. Everything seemed normal until a sudden scream tore through the basement—a girl's voice, crying out in sheer pain and terror. Her screams grew louder and more agonising. People rushed to the door and tried to open it, but it was locked from the inside. The girl couldn't open it. Her pain was in her loud and horrible screams. She didn't stop screaming, louder and louder, and then... it was all dead silent.

Then someone in the crowd began calling out a name— "Scully!" No one knew who Scully was. The person ran upstairs and returned with that tall, bald man with a cut on his neck. He had no name; he was named 'Scully' for some reason by that person.

The man requested Scully to break the door and asked the others to stand behind him with anything they could use as weapons. Scully threw his weight against the door and broke the lock. When they peered inside, the girl was nowhere to be seen. Scully noticed a piece of cloth on the floor. He picked it up and immediately threw it away when he realised it was a little girl's dress. Just then, they saw something move beneath the toilet seat cover. Panic broke out—they all fled the washroom, locked the door from the outside, and sealed it after spraying poison inside to kill whatever creature was inside—now larger and stronger than before.

And once again, they chose to hide the incident from Arthur and Bella. When Caller came to know about this brutal death through Neviah who had witnessed it, she felt sorry for the little innocent girl. Caller was expecting nothing more and nothing less after seeing people's act the night before last.

She was well aware that Arthur and Bella would come to know about it sooner or later, so with a heavy heart, she made up her mind— it was time to tell them everything.

Bella was with Arthur in the control room when Caller quietly called her out, making sure Arthur didn't notice. She managed to take Bella into a separate room to talk. There, Caller told her everything—from the discussions of the night before last, to the digging in the basement yesterday morning, and finally, the horrific incident in the washroom that morning. Her words shook Bella to her core, like the ground had slipped from beneath her. Her heartbeat soared. She could only listen. Nothing came to her mind. Her mind froze. It took her a few moments to even process what she was hearing. For a moment, it felt like a nightmare she couldn't wake up from. She was trying not to believe it. The more Caller revealed, the more disbelief and fury welled up inside her. Before Caller could finish her last sentence, Bella bolted—racing toward the stairs and down into the basement.

People stood close to one another, somber and silent. The dead girl's mother was crying out loud. Bella slowly walked toward the washroom, now locked and sealed with tape and plastic sheets. The smell near the washroom was unpleasant.

Bella looked around in horror—at each and every demon's faces disguised themselves as humans, wearing crocodile's tears in their eyes. The mother of the girl sobbing hard looked no less than a demon to Bella. They all were to blame. Each and every.

"We denied! Again and again! We refused to dig the ground! We said it because we knew, actually, we used our common sense and thought if the trees died and the water got so much worse that it started smelling, it was of course because of the soil; the ground. The Earth has died not just from the outside but from the inside. We are trying to do every possible thing to make all of us get safe to Mars but, you... you... and you" she shrieked, pointing her finger at their faces, horridly. "Each of you are doing nothing but making things worse for us now," shrieked Bella louder. Her face grew red with fury. She could no longer bear to look at their ugly and dumb faces.

Bella tied her hair back tightly, then turned to Caller. "Who dug the ground, Caller?" she asked coldly.

"The man with the tape in his hand," Caller replied.

It was Scully.

He looked directly at Caller. Bella stepped forward, eyes locked on him. "Look here," she said, walking up to him with a faint smile. Slowly, she pulled her hand from her pocket, arms crossed over her chest, and said in a low and seething voice, "I promise, if anything goes wrong with another kid or if they get hurt, I won't regret once to be the reason for your death." Caller quickly stepped forward, placed a hand on her shoulder, and started to make her walk out.

"Use your useless strength for something good, and do not bother this thing up in your head," said Bella as they climbed the last few flights of stairs.

"What are you doing?" Bella snapped, shaking Caller's hand off.

"What am I doing? Didn't you see in his eyes? He was almost in for a punch on your face" shrieked Caller and stormed away.

Bella stood still, then raised her voice to reach it to Caller, "A punch won't do justice to what I'll do to him if anything happens to my children. And I promise that."

She turned and made her way to the control room to Arthur. When she reached the floor, she saw him outside the room, leaning against the wall for support, a book in his hand.

"Arthur," she called out, "there is a problem downstairs in the basement."

Arthur looked up. "Well, Bella, we've a bigger problem here, the system has shut down on its own," said Arthur and stepped away from the wall and stood upright. "I was hoping you could take a look and help Neviah fix it. He's in there."

Bella hesitated, then said, "People dug the ground yesterday morning. And all they found were insects in the dead soil." Bella simply waited for his reaction.

Arthur's face tensed. "Please tell them to stop messing with things around. I hope nothing serious happened?"

"A little girl is dead. They say the insects were bigger and stronger than the ones they saw before. They've sealed the washroom and sprayed poison, but... I doubt if we are safe."

They both were clueless. Things got much worse in a short time, they had no idea how and what to react to. The feeling of being left out on the planet home to death was killing people more than before. The silence had caught up with everything for a moment when finally the machines started beeping again and Neviah shouted with excitement. He danced around the room and Bella and Arthur too joined him in the celebration. The machines were fully working. Arthur went near the machine and tried to read the texts on it.

"Does it say, connect to Mars?"

"Yes!"

Arthur glanced at Bella and then turned to Neviah and asked amusingly, "What are you waiting for exactly?" They all laughed in joy and glanced at each other with eyes full of water. Their happiness was immense, reflected in their cheerful faces.

Neviah pressed the button, and the screen went blank once.

One, Two, Three, Four, Five... (machine beeping)

[Six Months Earlier]

There was a boy named Harley. He was sobbing and murmuring under the blanket. He then stood up and wiped his tears, rubbing his face so hard that his eyes turned red. In the early dawn, his hair looked blue and red, and his eyes were shining. He took a shower, wore a black t-shirt and black jeans, then took a deep breath. Sitting on a chair with his journal, he began to write:

I hate my parents. They hated me all the time, all my life. At the age of eighteen, I moved to California and started working as a waiter in a big restaurant. I had visions of the Apocalypse. I saw aliens in my visions. There was a big crisis in people's lives—people running from one street to another, from one city to another, one country to another. Screams of anger. Crying men and women. The air was polluted. The solid was dead. No one was left on Earth.

Some had colonised Mars. leaving nothing behind.

A few days later, I had another vision—of aliens again. It was raining blood when they came to Earth.

I'm afraid the aliens are following me. I feel them everywhere, all the time.

This morning, when I watched the news, I realised my visions were true.

In my dream, I saw a man standing outside a car, crying and shouting his daughter's name. He fell to the ground, then started dragging himself along the dirt, searching for her dead body.

There were thousands of corpses.

"Amanda, my daughter! Amanda! What happened to you? I'm here, can you see me? Hey, my child..." the man sobbed when he finally saw his daughter.

He removed his safety mask, kissed his daughter, and hugged her.

Then I saw a woman—not too old—standing behind him. She stared at him with furious eyes and shouted, "Wear your mask back, you idiot!"

She screamed again, telling him to save his own life and stop acting stupid.

But then she realised... She was in danger too. The man had already been exposed to the air.

She stepped back. As she was about to turn, she saw the man slowly rise. His skin began to pale. His hair fell out. Within a minute, his skin started to fall out. The woman screamed in horror. The man grew worse by the second—until he looked inhuman. When he turned around, his eyes were bleeding. His face looked like a burned potato.

Dear reader,

The most horrific thing on Earth is Nature. It is the most beautiful, but also the most dangerous. And we humans are provoking it.

Six, Seven, Eight, Nine, Ten... connecting. [Machine beeping]

"Hello, can you hear us?" Arthur emphasised every word loudly.

"Is this Arthur?" asked the voice from the machine.

"This is. This is Dr. Arthur, calling from Earth," said Arthur. "Please help us, we are trapped here."

"Hello, Dr. Arthur. This is Carl from the NASA team. We have something to say before you tell us anything or the connection disconnects again," said Carl in a hurried voice.

"Okay!"

"Tomorrow is the full Moon on Earth. On the full Moon, there's going to be blood rain and the aliens will arrive. It's difficult to believe, but we found it in someone's journal. His mother stole it from him when she last saw him, and we came across it just a few days ago.

We can't ignore the details given in the journal, it's better to prepare ourselves. We need to be ready—for a big run. Aliens are deaf, as far as we know—or at least, the rain might make it hard for them to hear us.

We're not sure about any of this, but I assure you, Dr. Arthur, we'll be there tomorrow and help everyone get to Mars. We'll arrive at night. Please make sure everything goes well until we come."

"Thank you so much, Carl," said Arthur with joy. "Please keep contacting us."

[Call hangs up automatically.]

Arthur took off his hat and almost cried as he looked at Bella, who smiled and wrapped her arms around him in a tight, heartfelt hug. Neviah greeted them both with joy and excitement and left from there to share the news with Caller.

Arthur put his hat back on, "We should tell the people."

"Yes," Bella agreed.

Arthur walked out of the room. He looked down at the ground floor where people were walking side to side—some already watching him. The noise faded as Dr. Arthur and Bella were seen together. As everyone gathered and turned their eyes to Arthur for some news, Arthur announced out loud with joy, "We did it!"

And people whistled, shouted and laughed out of joy, jumped and danced around. Some started to cry. Then, everyone started to sing his name loudly and enthusiastically, "Arthur! Arthur! Arthur!"

"Now?" asked Arthur. "Should we talk about aliens too?"

"I think we should hold that. Maybe save it for tomorrow," said Bella. "Let people celebrate today."

"Good idea. Well, okay then," smiled Arthur. "I'm tired. I think I'll rest the whole day today."

"You should! I'm tired too."

Bella went to her left and Arthur to his right. The machines kept running, beeping steadily. People continued to jump with joy, telling their children stories about Mars—what it would look like.

But as the hours passed, joy began to give way to worry. Would Mars really send help? Would they survive the journey?

Some stared at the walls in silence, while others slowly drifted off to sleep—dreaming of a tomorrow still unknown.

Time passed quickly, yet slowly too— for some.

It was late evening, and most people hadn't eaten, consumed instead of anger and frustration. Arthur lay on his bed, immersed in a book, when Neviah entered the room. He stood silently for a moment, waiting to be noticed, then cleared his throat with a subtle but deliberate sound.

Arthur looked up, raised his eyebrows, set the book aside and gestured for him to sit.

"Dr. Arthur, we've got a problem," said Neviah, slightly out of breath.

"Where, Neviah? The control room?" panicked Arthur.

"Not with machines, but—"

"Neviah," Arthur interrupted sharply, "next time if you have bad news, say it directly." His tone was firm but not loud. "Now tell me, what happened?"

"I thought you already told everyone about the aliens, so I—"

"So you told them," Arthur snapped. "And I can imagine how you've panicked over something so small."

"I was just trying to—"

"What's bothering you so much, Neviah?" Arthur softened his tone, almost like speaking to a child. "We don't have everything under our control. We've helped them with all we could. We're scientists and doctors, not their grandfathers—we can't protect them like a shield."

Neviah fidgeted. "But they're neither eating nor letting others eat."

"And why is that?"

"Some of them are saying it's useless to keep hoping, and they'd rather die before the aliens eat them."

Arthur let out a short laugh and leaned forward. "Didn't you tell those fools that aliens don't eat humans or anything at all?"

Neviah gave a faint smile. "They won't listen now. It's out of control, and the bigger, stronger ones are making it worse."

"I don't care anymore. Let them do what they want," Arthur muttered, exasperated. "Just make sure Bella and her children get food. That's all I ask."

"Yes, sir."

Neviah left in silence. Arthur picked up his book again. Though unable to concentrate, he forced himself to read each paragraph multiple times until it began to make sense.

He kept reading for hours, then finally locked the door from inside before lying down. He was afraid now—afraid of the people—and unsure how far their foolishness could go.

The day had finally arrived.

The day everyone had longed for—the day they would fly to Mars. But since last night, the mood had changed. No one seemed excited anymore; they only hoped for a peaceful death. The children, while almost unaware of the full situation, had sensed something terribly wrong.

Parents were tired of pretending everything was normal. The chatter, the laughter, the play—every comforting sound had been buried under a thick blanket of anxiety and despair. Windows had become their only connection to the outside world—a world that was now completely destroyed. There was no place left untouched by the virus in the air.

A few good people still held on to hope. They believed they would make it out. They tried to comfort others, but most had already given up. The ones who had destroyed the food in panic or selfishness now kept to themselves, too ashamed to speak. They watched from afar as the hopeful ones quietly helped each other, shared whatever was left, and tried to keep the children calm. Guilt weighed heavily on the guilty, yet none of them dared to apologise or join the group again—they knew they had crossed a line that couldn't easily be undone.

But at the end they were still family, all living under the same roof. But most of all, the worries were for children. There were not much food left. Bella, too, had little food left in her room—but it was enough to feed her children a decent breakfast.

CHAPTER FOUR

THE LAST DAY

Bella spent her early morning with her children—playing and talking. When they grew tired, she left the room with a kiss and headed downstairs to her friend. She knocked on his door. He opened it with a smile, welcoming her inside.

"Were you sleeping?" Bella asked as she made herself comfortable on a chair.

"No... no. I was reading a book, actually. Actually... I'm kind of trying to write a book too," Arthur said, his words slightly hesitant, as if they didn't want to come out but did anyway.

"When? When did you think of that? This is amazing! I'm really keen to read your book. Wow!" Bella thumped the table in excitement and laughed.

"I never wanted to tell you about it. But—"

"But why?"

"Because when you tell people, they start expecting too much from you. So much that they believe whatever you write will win an award or something. They don't say it directly, but that's how it feels when they constantly appreciate you and push you to do more—hoping you'll write something great one day. And deep down, you know it probably won't happen," Arthur explained, his voice low and honest. "It gets even harder when that person is someone close to you. Like you. As you said… well… I was even thinking of publishing it under a pseudonym, but not under my own name. I don't even know if I'll be able to finish it. I think it'll end up being just a short article or a paragraph. I was too excited to write it, so I started, but now I have no idea where it's going. Whatever I write loses meaning after a while." He sat on a chair facing Bella—not directly in front of her—and finally glanced up at her after pouring out his thoughts.

Bella kept a small smile on her face, listening as she leaned slightly on the table, waiting for Arthur to continue. She was a close friend of his and had spent a significant part of her life with him, yet she had never seen this side of Arthur—nervous and insecure. And oddly, she felt good seeing this other part of him.

"You know, I feel like I'll disappoint everyone I know," Arthur said, glancing at her with a tight smile. "Either by writing something that's not good enough, or by writing something so honest—so full of my ideas and opinions—that they won't like it. It feels like… if I don't write anything, at least they'll respect me for who they think I am. But if I write something, I might lose even that. And yet, not writing… it doesn't feel good either."

"I've always wanted to share something with you too," Bella said thoughtfully, leaning back in her chair. "You always asked me if I was happy in life, and I always told you I was. I was not. My husband and I used to fight about everything. There was a time I was genuinely happy and believed I'd do something great. But then we met and got married. He made me feel guilty for being myself, and eventually, I started hating everything—including my children. They felt like a burden."

She paused for a moment, her eyes distant.

"When he died, I wasn't happy... but I wasn't sad either. Since he's been gone, the responsibilities have grown, but I handle them on my own now—and I do it happily. I want the best of my children now, and then for myself. I believe life is about living it. It's not about constantly thinking, worrying, or questioning. I'm not trying to lecture you—I just want you to think about it."

Bella leaned forward again, smiling with a spark of playful excitement. "It's just like when your classmates used to make your fun in the science lab and didn't believe in your work but you'd always say, 'I don't care.'"

"Is it the same thing?" Arthur chuckled.

"Don't overthink. It is the same. People will always have opinions. You do what you do. And if you ever need help with your book, I'd love to help."

"Okay! I'll come to you if I need."

"Perfect."

"Knock, knock," came a voice from the door. Neviah stepped in, followed by Caller. Both smiled. They looked exactly the same as when Bella had first met them—tall and sweet. As always, they moved quickly with their long, thin legs and greeted Bella and Arthur with a cheerful "Good morning!"

"So, this is our last day on Earth. We might never see it again," Neviah said, his face glowing with excitement.

"Yeah," Bella and Arthur said at once.

"How's the day outside?" Arthur asked, frowning slightly.

"The usual," Neviah replied. "The sun is burning like fire, and it seems like the bricks of this building have even started to decompose."

He stepped forward, gripping the back of a chair for support as he leaned slightly toward Arthur. "So... do we really have anything to fear from the aliens, sir?"

"I don't know," Arthur admitted. "But it's possible the aliens are afraid of us too—because neither side knows what the other is truly capable of. Still, if they manage to reach Earth, that already proves they're more advanced than us—in technology, knowledge, and maybe even physically. I'm not sure about the last one."

He continued, "The farthest we've travelled from Earth is just over five hundred thousand miles. If aliens can travel much farther, then they're clearly more dangerous. They might even try to establish their own civilisation here—and thanks to us, they'd have it easy.

He looked around the room. "Now, it's not just that we need to escape. We must. If even one human remains visible to them, we could all be at risk. Today might be the last—but most important—day of our lives. We've survived this long. Now we have to fight for each other.

"But how do we protect ourselves?" Caller interrupted.

Arthur frowned. "What do you mean?"

"How do we know what precautions to take? What exactly should we avoid? We need to make sure we leave no trace of humans. After all, if the aliens are here to destroy us, they'll be looking for any sign of life. And if the stories are true, they absorb energy from their surroundings to power themselves."

"You're right," Arthur said, growing more serious. "We have to be careful—especially with the dangers we already know about."

It was midday. Arthur, along with Bella, Neviah, and Caller, went back to work. There wasn't a single person on the ground floor. They moved through each room, searching for anything that was needed or could be used, and placed the items outside. They had to ensure there were enough safety suits to get everyone from the building to the spaceship safely. But it turned out—not everyone could be saved.

There were one hundred and four safety suits. A large number, yes, but still not enough. After Cassandra counted everyone at Bella's request, three people were left without suits.

They all asked the same question: "What should we do now?"

While everyone was stressed, Arthur tried to calm them, assuring them they would find a way.

Three people—it was a big number. No one wanted to lose anyone; all of them were connected, bound by some relationship or bond.

Arthur needed fresh ideas, so he asked Cassandra to join and help design a suit that could block the air. Now, those who had destroyed the food the previous night—and in doing so, made everyone lose hope—were filled with guilt and shame.

As time passed, more people came downstairs and asked if they could help. They all worked together, offering different ideas. But nothing worked. They lacked the tools and equipment, and what little progress they made wasn't enough.

Then, unexpectedly, Caller came up with a new problem—not a solution to the existing one. While Arthur and the others were deep in their work, Caller approached Arthur, looking down, and asked with a furrowed brow, "Dr. Arthur... isn't light also a problem for us?"

Arthur glanced at her briefly, looked around, and then walked away from the others. Caller followed him proudly, and Arthur snapped, irritated,

"I know what you're talking about, okay? But I think there's a bigger problem right here. The light's not that bright here—it's not noticeable from outside."

Caller noticed the hardness in his tone, though it wasn't necessary. Still, she smiled and said gently, "But sir, it'll be dark outside at night. So, even a small or dim light will be noticeable, right? And—"

"So what do you want me to do!?" Arthur burst out.

He recoiled, stepping back, and once again took off his hat, completely unaware of how sudden his reaction had been. He looked around, slightly embarrassed. But people, sensing his anger, quickly resumed working, pretending they hadn't seen or heard anything.

Arthur turned and walked upstairs, his expression terrible. Though he seemed calm on the outside, he was growing more and more irritable inside. His temper was no longer under control, and he had started panicking over the smallest things. It made him feel bored, sad, and exhausted. Bella, too, had begun worrying about his health. But she decided to leave him alone for a while and threw herself back into her work.

In her mind, she thought Arthur would call for her soon, but she also knew she wouldn't go. She had too many things to do, and time was running out.

Meanwhile, Caller stood motionless, watching Arthur until he disappeared. Her eyes were heavy and wet. She looked around, but then Neviah approached her, smiling as if nothing had happened.

He gently held her face in his hands, looked into her eyes, and almost whispered, "Nothing happened. Everything is fine, okay?"

He kissed her forehead.

Caller looked around again, her eyes filled with disappointment and hopelessness. She didn't say anything. She wasn't angry at Arthur, nor sad that he had yelled.

She was heartbroken because the man who had always helped others with enthusiasm now looked like he had lost all hope.

She felt that the building was no longer a safe place.

The hurried footsteps of workers and the silent glances of children, who should have been playing, made her realise that even if everything seemed fine for now, it would all go to waste in the end.

After a few moments of silence between them, Caller finally asked, her voice heavy, "I'm tired... can I just rest for a while?"

Neviah didn't reply. He simply picked her up in his arms—as if something in him had needed to do that—and carried her into a room so she could rest.

After they left, Bella asked Cassandra to keep an eye on the people and ensure that everything went well. Then, she made her way to see Arthur.

She looked through every room—even the control room—where the machines were still running and making sounds, luckily. On the screen, texts lit up in green, and graphs showed network connectivity, data transfer speed, weather conditions, radar information, and more. It was warm near the machines.

After that, she went into the room where she had been staying with her children. There, she found him laughing and talking with them. Arthur was sitting on the table, while the children sat on the sofa.

"Mommy!" the girl shrieked with joy as she noticed Bella enter, while the boy simply grinned at his mother. Bella smiled and joined them, gleefully holding her children's hands in her fists. The girl giggled sweetly, covering her mouth with her small hands, and everyone laughed—if only because of the joy in her expression and the sounds she made.

Her brother, by contrast, was the quiet one. He wasn't shy, but he preferred not to speak much. He simply liked to listen.

Bella looked at Arthur and smiled, though she wasn't sure what to say. Questions had been dangling in her mind since she'd visited the control room and seen the machines. Before she could speak, Arthur looked at her and asked,

"Did you really name the kids Girl and Boy?"

Bella had been asked this question many times before, the month after Boy was born. She always felt a sense of pride in her voice when answering, though she never fully understood why. Still, she was happy with it—so much so that when Girl was born, she named her without hesitation, even though her husband had insisted on giving her a more conventional name.

She vividly remembered the moment when he screamed at her, telling her to stop her nonsense. But Bella found those names not only acceptable, but good—endearing, even.

Yet, this time, when Arthur asked the question, it struck her differently. It sounded strange.

Why does it feel like a bird in a coffin? she wondered. She struggled to find her words for a moment, but soon realised it wasn't strange at all—not to her.

She glanced at her children, then looked back at Arthur and replied, "Yes, I did. And I think these are unique names—just like my children are to me."

Arthur didn't try to say something to please her. But his response was so sincere that he stood up from the table, ruffled both Girl's and Boy's hair, and said naturally, "I believe they'll do something great someday."

CHAPTER FIVE

THE BIG NIGHT: SUICIDE OF A HOPE

Arthur and Bella talked about everything they could, and slowly, the conversation turned toward their college days. The children grew more and more interested, eager to hear the stories of their lives.

They reminisced about how, back in college, one of them would fall in love with someone new almost every month—only to end it if the other disapproved. It had been fun back then, full of silly rules and laughter. But as they kept talking, the story reached the part where Bella met her husband—and suddenly, everything went quiet.

Oh Lord, Bella cried out silently in her mind.

Breaking the silence, Girl jumped onto the sofa and asked, "What happens next?"

Arthur smiled.

"Next," he began warmly, "after one semester, your father met your mother. He was tall and handsome. Not in the same class as your mom, but after a few months, he changed a few subjects just to be with her— just to sit beside her in class. He was a good guy. But then…"

Arthur, now seated on the table with his legs crossed, took off his hat and placed it in his lap. He continued:
"I met your father in college. He really was a decent guy. We used to talk quite often. Things were going well—until I got into a fight with one of his friends. That day… things started to fall apart. I fought with your father too. And your mom—she decided to end it all. Our years of friendship.

"It was never the same after that. We stopped talking. We avoided each other. And then, I dropped out of college… for other reasons."

He paused and realised that he was interacting with children. For a moment the room held its breath. Arthur continued to simply complete the story.

"I met your mother again seven or eight years later, right Bella?! At a hospital, yeah. We were working together. By then, I was already planning to leave. I didn't want to spend my life doing surgeries and MRIs. I had other dreams. I was still young and restless."

Arthur's voice softened and continued with more excitement in his voice.

"I wanted something more—something that kept my mind alive. Something… energetic. Enthusiastic.
And that's always been Astronomy. Since I was a child."

He emphasised the word Astronomy with a quiet reverence, as if it was not just a dream but the last flicker of something still burning inside him. "But, even if you love something more than anything in the world, some days you still feel bored or low. Over time, I've come to think that it's normal. Those days actually make you love it more—because when you go looking for joy elsewhere and find nothing that excites you like your true passion does, you come back to it. And boom, now you love it more than ever. So yeah... those awful days are important too."

Bella had grown a little emotional—for reasons even she couldn't fully explain. A quiet wave of self-blame crept in. She believed that the reason their friendship broke back then was because of her. Her thoughts flickered between guilt and the painful memory of telling her children about their father's death.

She had told them directly, bluntly—as if informing them about the death of some distant relative. When he died, he was in another city, far from his family. Bella had wanted to see him one last time. She had loved her husband more than anyone else in her life. But over time, that love had become like a twinkling star in the night sky—beautiful, distant, and fading.

Sometimes, when her children asked if she had loved their father, she wouldn't know how to respond—or whether there even was a right answer.

Arthur instantly regretted how he had told the story—as if he had indirectly blamed Bella for what happened in the past. In his view, maturity is understanding what love truly is and how we express it. And maybe, just maybe, he would have done the same as Bella if he had found his love.

His younger self had been disappointed—with friends, with family, with his long and stagnant career. That frustration had made him irritable, closed-off, and unable to share his inner world with anyone. It was one of the reasons he had remained single.

Silence had caught the room again as if the silence outside the building was showing its effect on the walls. The kids were watching Arthur. His legs swayed side to side in a funny rhythm. They smiled when his eyes met theirs.

Bella, meanwhile, sat with her legs crossed, leaning forward slightly. She rested her elbow on her raised knee and cradled her chin in her palm. Her thoughts had drifted again—to the machines, to the control room.

The machines were working fine. The screen showed they had been running for several hours. She worried they might shut down again but hesitated to say anything to Arthur. She knew that if the machines kept running, people on Mars could detect their current, live location—which could greatly improve the chances of saving lives.

She was afraid of how Arthur would react if the machines failed again after such promising news.

But it's impressive, she thought. At least for us, the machine worked. And it's still working after all this time. But how is that possible? Did it correct itself somehow?

Her mind swirled with questions. She wanted to share them with Arthur—but held back. Maybe now wasn't the time.

As they all sat quietly, lost in thought, someone knocked at the door.

It was Cassandra.

"A lady wants to go out, sir," cried Cassandra.

"Where? Again? Where wants she go?" asked Arthur.

"She wants to go out? And why is that?" asked Bella.

"Sir, Ma'am, you may want to talk to her. I have no idea why she says that, but she wants to meet you as well, sir, before she goes out," told Cassandra in one breath.

"O! What is it? Is it worse than living here isolated?" grumped Arthur in disbelief. He then used one hand bracing on the table's edge, the other gently cradling his knee, and stood with extreme weariness on his face.

Arthur, along with Bella, walked down to the ground floor while the children stayed up there and watched them from the walkway. When Arthur reached there, people were already circling the woman. Neviah too arrived there along with Caller and brought a chair for Arthur to sit. And then it began. Arthur took a deep breath, hoping it wouldn't be too long and serious, and listened.

"Sir, I wanted to meet you for the last time. I respect you and I admire you because of what you do and what you have done for us. You helped us, and you have inspired me several times in my life by doing things that most people get afraid of, or they doubt themselves—that things that couldn't have been done by most people can't be done by anyone. But the doubt and people that I'm talking about, I'm one of them, and I'm troubled with myself. I don't see any life anywhere, and so I want to go out and die myself. You helped all of us and will continue, but I give up. I give up. I just give up. Uh! Life, life, life—this life," sobbed the lady. She spoke in a dead voice while saying the word life, and almost cried.

Arthur looked calmly at the lady and said, "Well, it's every one of us that is helping each other, and what you are going to do is not a help to us. So, I want you to stay here and help us. We all want you to stay here, and you will be saved, and then you can start a new life."

"I do not want to start a new life. I don't want to live any minute longer. I told you I'm bored of living."

Bella looked at the lady, not understanding her or the words she said. "So?"

"She is the mother of the daughter who died of insects in the washroom," said Neviah.

"So?" Bella kept the same expression on her face and then looked at the lady and said, "Madam, you can't go out and take your life just on your wish. I ask you not to do any such thing that might become a danger for all of us here."

"You don't command me!" shrieked the lady in pain and started to cry. "I had lost my whole family in just a matter of days a few months ago. I was here with my only daughter, my love of life and the only star of my eyes, but now she is gone too. Now, since she was the star of my eyes, how can this eye possibly be bright again? I see only darkness, but nothing much more than that, and nothing much left too—to live."

Caller walked forward a little and said, "It's a bad phase for all of us here, and no one really seems to be happy here—lonely and isolated—but we need to go through it. I also lost my father some days ago before I came here. Time shall pass. It will pass for you too."

Bella meanwhile watched the lady and grew more irritated—not for any other reason but by the fact that while all of them were trying to find ways to save the lives of each other, the lady was wasting their time, not helping but creating a probability of bad consequences by her actions. There was not much time left, as it flies on Earth now. It was already late afternoon, and things were not getting much better here, but the only hope there was—that we had—had now been put on the sword.
"So, what do you want us to do, die here?"

"I don't want anything, and I don't want you people to do anything either. We won't make it long on Mars, so it's all in vain to try to settle there on Mars, because ultimately, it's all gone in the air, and when breathed in, this air makes you not happy, but instead only makes you sad—remembering all the efforts we made," sobbed the lady and fell on the ground, holding her eyes in her palms.

Cassandra walked near the lady and said, "But sister, it's better to do something than to do nothing in the hope that we will be saved somehow. Believe me, sister, you aren't the only one going through these tragic events of life. I pray for your daughter's soul to rest in peace, and I pray for you too—to live your life for your daughter."

The lady stopped sobbing and locked her eyes on the ground for a while, and then she took a deep breath. Soaking her tears under her finger's skin, she looked at Arthur. The lady gazed at Arthur and said, "Sir, give me the permission to go now. Hereafter, I will look after myself."

"You can go. If this is your wish and if this is what you want. But remember—it's not my wish to let you go, but my compulsion, while you leave me with no other choice."

"Yes, I know, Arthur. Indeed, it is my will," said the lady, and before she could utter further words, Arthur said, "Ma'am, before you go, I want to let you know that we aren't really sure about the virus—if it really affects the same way and not some other way. The virus might change from time to time, and it shouldn't be affecting the same as before. That means you might not directly get the death, but may endure its severe effects—and a death that comes unknown to death itself. It means you might go through several deaths before getting to the real one."

"You still wish to go out, ma'am?" asked Bella.

"Yes, I do," said the lady.

"Okay then!" said Arthur. "Let her go out, Neviah, and make sure you open the door the right way and close it too—the right way, as we do. And do mask your face and cover up your whole face, as there might be danger in each particle of air outside. Got that?"

"Got it, sir," said Neviah and walked into his room to grab a mask to cover up his face, while others were just astonished and simply looked at the lady in disbelief.

Caller, meanwhile, told them that she would look outside through the window to see how it is outside—as an excuse with no intention to do that, but simply wanted to be alone, and so she walked upstairs into a room. When Neviah came back, his face had literally gone white for a while when he didn't see Caller there, but by then he had realised where she might have gone.

Neviah went near Arthur and said in a low voice, "Sir, I'm afraid for Caller. She has been having some anxiety for the last few hours, and I can't leave her alone for even a few minutes, as it might not be good for her. I will be quick and be right here in a few minutes. May I leave now? I want a few words with her. I will be right back."

"Be fast."

Neviah ran upstairs quickly, holding his face mask in his hands, and looked for the room where Caller was. After checking a few rooms, he finally found Caller sitting on one of the chairs surrounding a dining table. She was there, laying her hands on the table and resting her head on them. "Are you okay, Caller?" asked Neviah sweetly, and sat beside her, leaving one chair between them.

Caller didn't say anything but looked into his eyes while lying with her head on the table and smiled graciously.

"Why are you up here?" Neviah posed another question to her.

Caller smiled again and lifted her head, supporting her chin with one hand. She gazed into his eyes and said, "I won't mind."

"You won't mind what?" laughed Neviah.

"If you sit closer," answered Caller.

"You are being cheesy," chuckled Neviah and moved over to the chair right next to her. "Overdramatic."

Neviah put his hand around Caller's waist and held her tight. Caller made no effort to free herself and stayed close to his chest, where she felt warm and safe, as if it was all she wanted—to live in his arms forever, gazing into each other's eyes and talking of love, but nothing else.

"Neviah, don't leave me now. I want to sit here with you, holding hands, and never leave this seat," Caller spoke of love with a sweet and lovely voice.

"I won't," said Neviah, looking directly into her lovely and true eyes of love as they sparkled in the room's dim light. "Arthur is calling me. I need to leave."

"Don't go, I request!"

"I'm confused if I'm talking to Caller. Why do you act so strange sometimes?" smiled Neviah and kissed her on the forehead. "I love you. I'm all yours. Give me five minutes, and I'll be right back here with you, sitting with you on one chair."

"You can go, but then there's no need to come back in urgency. I will wait," said Caller with a sad heart.

"Say it simply," urged Neviah.

"We don't use common sense or social or personal etiquette when we're deeply in love with somebody, do we? In love, we go mad and sometimes crazy, don't we?" Caller then hugged Neviah tightly and continued, "The seconds on a clock that go tick, tick, tick feel like years when waiting for love. Time becomes an enemy in love as it goes quicker, and a friend in solitude, where its leisurely pace offers solace and reflection."

Neviah gently held her neck with both hands, delicately easing out of the hug. His touch was tender as he created space to catch a glimpse of her face. He looked into her eyes, grinned, and promised, "I'll be right back!" After a while, staring into each other's eyes, Neviah laughed out loud.

"What?" he said and continued laughing. But she stifled his laugh with her lips.

"Okay! Now I have to, have to go!" Neviah smiled graciously and kissed her again. "Arthur calls me again!"
As Neviah was leaving, Caller kissed him full on the lips again and smiled. Neviah smiled too and left the room.

While all of them down on the ground floor were waiting for Neviah, Bella thought of something else. To discuss it, she went near Arthur and said in a low voice, "Arthur, do we really need to do it? I mean, we could simply tie up the lady to something and keep her in a room. I know it would be wrong, but it's better than taking the risk of opening the door and putting all of our lives in danger. What if she doesn't die and becomes a problem for us while we wait here for the spaceship?"
Arthur looked at Bella and said, "But I have already explained to you that the air outside couldn't damage anything inside the building, so don't worry about that. No matter what it is outside, as long as it's only the virus in the air, this building won't let anything happen to us. And what do I say about the lady—I think it's written in her destiny. She'll go."
[Aside] "Let it happen, Bella. Let it happen, for this is what I want now—to see what the air holds now, or if even the air has left the Earth."

As Neviah reached downstairs, he graciously instructed the lady to come to the door and asked her to come with him. The others were staring at the situation, carrying no sympathy toward the woman but only growing excitement and nervousness with every passing second. Their eyes were almost plucked out, and everyone stood there clenching their fists inside their pockets, waiting to see the lady walk outside while holding their breath.
Although there were a few who were not taking the situation very seriously, they still waited for it to happen

quickly so they could look away and focus on other things, as always.

Neviah, along with the lady, reached the door. Then, he opened it. The door opened, and people saw the sun running toward the west. Arthur looked at the nearly setting sun as if it, too, was leaving the Earth forever and realised how important the sun had now become for every one of them. The rays were not too bright, and the sun seemed to be covered under a cloak like a witch, cursing the Earth and leaving it with a bad note. Bella looked at the sun—exhausted, it appeared—as though it had ceased to shine.

A few more seconds passed, and the lady glanced back and looked emotionally. But Neviah tried to push the door a little harder with every passing moment, urging it to close. The lady disappeared the very next moment as the door slammed hard and closed.

Everyone went inside the rooms along with their children. Parents of young children were gathered in one room, trying to make their children fall asleep, while the adults were having serious conversations with their parents in another room. In the lobby then, a few people were left: Arthur and Bella, Neviah and Caller, including Cassandra and those two big, bulky men whom almost everyone had been hating since late morning. Neviah walked slowly, head down, to his girlfriend Caller and stood there, hands in his pockets. Caller looked at him and asked if he was alright, to which Neviah nodded, took a glance at her, and gave a quick smile.

Arthur was still gazing at the door. He thought about the woman and remembered her eyes and the look she had in them. He then remembered his book, chair, and bed. He looked at Neviah and asked, "Are you good?"

Neviah looked straight and said gently, "Yes, sir."
Arthur then stood up from the chair and told Bella that he was going to his room and that he didn't want anybody to disturb him. As he was walking away, he looked back at Neviah and asked him, "Can you keep yourself up with the machine?"
"Yes, sir," Neviah bowed his head a little.
"Don't call me 'sir' from now on. Call me by my name!" said Arthur in a quirky, orderly voice.

The evening was coming, and it was bringing darkness with it. Though the building was still a safe place for the people, except that there was not much food left and they were only living on fresh air and drinkable water, the virus had started to show its colour inside the building. It was not noticeable, but people were terrified from the inside. A woman had already given up, and parents, children, and all were playing, like, a game inside their heads of hide and seek. This hide-and-seek game had become nothing other than to say: hide to be saved, or if sought, meet demise. Everyone was tense and unsafe. The only hope was help from Mars, and if it got delayed even one minute beyond the time nature had decided for them, it would be a catastrophic moment for all of them — as half would die hopelessly and others would watch them. Also, they were not so sure if the building would last for a month more. Time around the walls, in corners, on the floor, beneath the surface, and possibly everywhere, felt as if it was flying. The trees inside the building were rather behaving oddly in relation to the nature of time. Where trees must grow with every passing moment — or must grow until they reach their time that takes death instantly — here, the trees had stopped their growth. These trees were green, healthy, and providing fresh air, but they had just stopped growing, as if nature itself had declined to follow nature's nature.

CHAPTER SIX

THE BIG NIGHT: SPACESHIP ARRIVAL

It was a dark night. Arthur was in his room lying on his bed, eyes closed and a book at rest on his body. Neviah and Caller were sitting next to the thick wall that was dividing two big rooms in which people were expressing their sorrow and hoping for God to save them as their last hope when the innovative and cleverest minds lost hope and extraordinary machines ahead of their time faltered. Bella was sitting in the somewhat central area of the ground floor on a chair that Arthur was sitting on earlier. It was not so long before a long, blood-curdling shriek opened Arthur's eyes and bound people's feet to the ground. It was a shriek of four to five children from the roof, two of whom were Bella's children. The girl and boy ran down to the ground floor along with other children to their mother, Bella. As Bella saw her children running toward her, she fell down on her knees to hug them and started crying upon watching her children cry. Seeing this, other children started to cry too and fell into their mothers' laps and in their arms. Seeing Bella and her children crying, Arthur immediately ordered Neviah to go see what was on the roof. Neviah ran upstairs and walked into Bella's room. Nothing was wrong with the room, but as he looked up to the glass roof, he recoiled, stepping one foot back. It was raining blood, and the roof was totally red; it was refreshing with a new layer of blood with every new wave of blood rain. Neviah ran down quickly and murmured what he saw in Arthur's ear.

"So the boy was right!" Arthur spoke in a subdued voice.

"The boy!?"

"The boy Harley, the one—" said Arthur.

"The one who was found with the umbrella?" interrupted Neviah. "But... but I thought they told us that they found it from a mother. How are you so sure it's his?"

"I am sure!" said Arthur deeply. "Didn't you hear them saying that they found it from a mother who stole that journal from her son back then?"

"I remember now," responded Neviah. "So, what should be done now? Should we still wait for them to come and save us? And will they come for sure? We don't know and haven't even been in contact since that last talk by any medium."

"Don't bother me with these stupid questions, Neviah," said Arthur with a trace of bitterness in his voice and continued, saying: "I am old now. Think for yourself, and it should be more of your responsibility to look after all these people, not me."

"Yes, sir."

Arthur got irritated for some reason and said in a harsh voice: "And why is it that you have not contacted them again since after that? Keep trying to get in contact with them, understood?"

"Yes, sir," said Neviah again and moved his head again up and down.

Arthur walked a little and imitated the phrases — yes sir — in a gruff and irked undertone, his voice a barely audible echo of the deferential words.

Neviah heard Arthur and didn't like this major change in him. Neviah had been noticing Arthur for the last few days — that he was growing grumpy a little more every day. But he couldn't do anything but listen and notice him. Arthur was old now, and it was typical to become aggressive over little things, though most of the old tend to become calm and loving. Neviah felt a little more responsibility on himself than before and a load on himself for the safety of people. As hope had already been hung on the gallows, it was the last chance to save all of their belief and them.

Things were happening as they were described in the diary. Although they were told it would be a blood rain, it didn't look like one. The ones who were curious enough to go upstairs and check on the rain were not really sure if it was blood rain, while others stayed down and didn't dare to move from their ground. Most who dared to go were men and some young boys. Even one of them — one who was large and bulky in size, bald and had a cut on his neck — went upstairs to see outside with his five-year-old son, whose mother passed away a long time ago when he was only seven weeks old. The rain was not a good view, as it was horrific for most of the people there.

The rain was continuously falling nonstop without any changes in the motion of its speed. And it was described as not a "blood rain" but simply the drops of water that were red in colour, dense and heavy. People were hoping things would turn out good at the end of the night and that the next morning would find themselves in a better place with other brothers of theirs on Mars. The sun was long gone and the dark had settled. The sky was neither blue nor any shade of dark; the moon was there in the sky, bright and glamorous.

But, as time passed with every breath of only a few people left on Earth, the dark seemed to conquer the moon. No clouds were there, but it was just that the Earth was welcoming no other outside guests. The clouds disappeared as there was no proper water or air or anything that was part of nature or life. Unaware to everyone, things did not stop worsening, as if there was no bound on anything as to what extent things could be awful that was left on the Earth. The Earth was getting worse day by day, but it was that now it was happening at a faster rate, and the Earth was under a rapid change every moment.

People were scared and no one wanted this type of death. They wanted to die better. People had better expectations from death too and wanted it in a better way but not this way. The night was becoming their lives' most important night and scary too. Everyone was trying their best to avoid causing any additional hustle and bustle around the building for Arthur, Bella, and Neviah. They stayed and moved as they were told. Everyone again was in those big two rooms on the ground floor and now no one was upstairs except Neviah. Arthur had not come out of his room since the last talk with Neviah and probably had locked his room from the inside; no one had checked on him. Bella too was on the ground floor in a room with her children and had refused to leave her children alone when Caller asked her to join him and Neviah to help them. But, while Caller had gone upstairs Bella had realised that it was more sensible to help them instead of sitting in a corner knowing that death was coming for all of them.

It was not so long after Caller went that Bella too headed toward the control room. She left her children in the room and without much talk (as there was not much time), she just told them to stay hidden in the room and hold each other's hands tight if they felt scared. Bella reached the control room but there was no one. The room was empty with machines and their slightly high beeping sounds that were continuously beeping in every second break. All lights were green on the machines and the system seemed to work properly and accordingly as it should've been. She didn't read the machines much and started to look for Neviah and Caller. She found them in the very next room to the control room where they were excitedly looking out of the glass roof and windows. First, she just looked at them for a short time and then gazed at Neviah's face and started to think about her husband and her younger days with him. She missed him. She wanted him near her in this difficult time. Suddenly, a bright, red light fell on Bella's face, waking her up from her thoughts and back to the room. Before she could react to anything, Caller turned to Bella, shouted in joy and said, "The spaceship has arrived!"

Bella for a moment didn't understand the words but looked at her face and then the words started coming into her mind, trying to make sense of the words 'arrived' and 'spaceship'. Bella was thrilled in joy and couldn't have described in words how happy she was but it was a joyful moment that seemed unreal. Bella ran to the window and saw this huge spaceship in size that all were waiting for over the last few months. The ship was long V-shaped, over fifty kilometers in length and ten in diameter. The front of the ship looked like a long V, and on the side of the middle were two wide U-shaped wings. The long V in the front was not sharp but a rough shape that was bright with yellowish light. In the middle, on the top of the ship was a beautiful small round glass that was bright with sky-blue light. Overall, the whole ship was bright with yellow light and sky-blue on the top. And so, the silver colour of the ship was also visible.

Things around the building seemed to happen so fast that it was almost unbelievable to any eye and for Bella, the spaceship was that thing that looked almost unreal. It was so huge in size that she felt a tiny body made up of tiny atoms in front of the ship. Even the building too was small. Bella didn't even realise but now she was alone in the room and both Caller and Neviah had left the room many moments ago to tell everyone about it. It was not possible that Bella could forget about her children in her astonishment at the size and shape of the ship but it was no wonder to lose one's consciousness after seeing the wonder and the beauty of the ship. Now as she was standing near the window, it was not possible for her to peer down at the street below. The window was peculiarly positioned—it sat tightly against the wall, angled upward toward the sky, although the sky was not a sky anymore or at least, it was not the same sky that the window was meant to fit. This unconventional placement made it impossible for Bella to look down around the building from the window. Bella was so lost that she didn't even notice the landing of the spaceship. And the spaceship was big enough that having the window directed toward the sky, Bella somehow was still able to gaze on the spaceship. Bella was not leaving the room and still then was lost in her own thoughts while Arthur too was in his room, uninformed, almost unconscious on his pills, lying on his bed and the book on his face, but the story must go on. And so, Neviah and Caller were doing their best to do things right and as it should be, things were going well under them.

While Caller was helping people to fit them into suits, Neviah was a little confused about how they would make it to the ship. He had a little idea about it but then it too was a failure as there were not enough suits so that they could have walked to the spaceship. He should've thought about it before, but as an excuse, he said to himself that he thought Mars probably had a solution for that as some of them, the people, on Mars knew exactly where people are trapped on Earth. Neviah was confused and so, the confused Neviah went near to Caller to tell her, he wanted to talk. They both walked away from people and as they were to start the conversation, they started hearing a loud noise (not too loud but instead a soft loud noise) beneath their feet. It continued for less than two minutes and then it stopped.

"What was that?" asked Caller.

"How do I know? I've no idea," answered Neviah.

"Are they digging under the ground?" asked Caller.

"Digging under the ground!?" exclaimed Neviah with uncertainty about what was said even means. "They'd only be doing it with some kind of tunnelling machine, but why are they digging?" he said finally, still uncertain.

"I'm sure they know that the soil is dead. Wait..." Caller stood silent for a moment and started to think. Neviah looked at her and said, interrupting her silence, "What?"

"Is there some kind of underground room that we aren't aware of?" said Caller instantly. "I mean, there might be."

"An underground room!?"

"Yeah! An underground room. Why don't you try to communicate with them over some kind of messages?" suggested Caller in a bit of a hurried voice.

"Right! They must have some kind of compact and portable device that can connect us to them even when they are on Earth, right?" asked Neviah.

"Right!" answered Caller.

"Right," said Neviah and ran upstairs into the control room while Caller was among the people. Just a minute passed and Bella too entered the control room and was surprised to see Neviah there. She walked a little toward the chair, and now Neviah was aware of her presence in the room, but he didn't really give much attention to her and kept pressing the keys on the keyboard, hard. Now Bella knew that Neviah knew that she was there. She kept silent for less than a moment and then finally spoke, "What are you doing here?"

"Nothing. I'm just—" Neviah stopped and again delved his eyes into the screen and fingers on the keys.

"I'm asking something!" said Bella in a bitter voice. "Where is everybody? Are they all still here? What's the plan? Is Arthur still in his room? Who's in charge, are you in charge of it?"

Bella's fury burned as intensely as the calmness of the situation. "Girl. Boy," she whispered and ran down as fast as she could. The door was opened exactly how she left it and she found her children in the same corner, sitting facing each other — one was even asleep. The boy was asleep and his head was on the girl's knee. It was then that her heart calmed. She exited the room without making any noise and headed toward Arthur's room first, but it was locked. She tried knocking, but he didn't answer, and it was quiet inside. Bella then tried to find Caller, and there she was, talking to Cassandra. Bella waved at Caller and called out to her. She walked with Cassandra.

"What is going on and what's the plan?" asked Bella.

"We don't have enough suits and so—" Caller's voice trailed off as Bella interjected and cried, "So what?"

"What do you mean by that?" asked Caller, annoyed.

"I mean, we already knew about it. There is nothing to discuss and nothing that we can do. Why wait?" said Bella in a not-so-pleasing tone.

"Don't bother yourself, Bella," spoke Cassandra, interfering between the two of them, trying to calm them down as they both seemed a little annoyed and angry. "Anyway, the suits that we have were never good enough to protect us — not all suits at least, I can say."

"We're trying our best, and you're supposed to help us," said Caller, out of nowhere, calmly. She tried to look calm too, but remained furious at Bella and didn't really seem to care about respecting her, but rather spoke to her with the same intensity of words as Bella did.

Bella ignored Caller completely and instead spoke with Cassandra and answered her by saying, "We must go along with what best we have, but if we don't have any better option than that, then it would be foolish to wait for death rather than try once to save ourselves."

Caller looked at Bella with one eye and desired to leave the conversation and get out of there so that she wouldn't have to see her face, but then she turned her face toward Cassandra and spoke, "Or sometimes we need to wait for some magic to happen — something that was always there, but we were too busy to see it. And sometimes, it's just always been hidden from us for the right reasons. Isn't that so, Cassandra?"

Cassandra looked helplessly at both of them. She turned to Bella and said excitedly, "We heard some sound underground, as if someone was drilling under the surface. Neviah and Caller estimate that it must be some kind of tunnelling machine, and—" she was interrupted.

"Don't mention names, Cassandra, it doesn't matter to her," said Caller in a very dramatic voice, trying to make Bella feel as if she was nothing, and that she and her lovely mate were the only ones doing the best possible. But somewhere back in her head, she couldn't ignore the fact that Bella was better than her — and indeed she was, she thought.

"Cuz it shouldn't be a matter, shall it?" asked Bella eagerly, and she really wanted an answer to this one. After a moment of silence, she continued, "Delving into the ins and outs of what was done and who was involved is an insignificant use of our valuable time." Her voice raised a little, not harder, but, said softly, "It mustn't be productive. Instead, we need to address the difficulties and problems at hand, disregarding any need for applause or recognition from others." She looked at Caller and continued, "particularly in the midst of adversity or when facing the demands of the battlefield." Bella finished with her words and the whole building was ghost-quiet. The whole Earth was ghost-quiet. It didn't last long before Bella spoke, "In simple words, what I want now is for you to continue, Cassandra. What were you saying?"

Cassandra looked at Bella with a smiley face and started again, "You were not here when it happened, but we all witnessed a loud noise as if tunnelling under the ground. The sound was not too loud, but it was loud enough that we were able to hear and feel it on the surface..." She paused and thought for a second and then continued again with one raised eyebrow, "And the reason the sound was not too loud was certainly because there's nothing left under the ground, except that what's left is the ash of soil."

Caller smirked.

"We wonder if there is an underground room. Do you know

anything about it?" asked Cassandra curiously.

"No, uhm... I... 've..." Bella's words scattered as she saw Neviah running wild downstairs. His face looked like a fresh blossoming sunflower. His eyes were wide in joy, and his mouth was open as if he had seen something terribly good. He had not stepped down all the stairs down the way, he cried loudly and joyfully, "We're saved! We are saved! We are safe now." He came nearer and nearer, and his hands went straight into his pants' pocket. He stood there, straight and tightened his body. He looked happier than anybody else there.

Caller came a little forward and asked enthusiastically, "Is there for real a room down the ground? And for real, are they coming to save us?"

"Yes! Yes, there is. And yes, they're waiting for us to come," answered Neviah quickly and looked at her nicely.

"Do we know now what that sound was?" asked Cassandra, a little concerned.

"You'll know. Walk with me down to the room, you'll know," said he.

Caller looked desperately left and right and asked, "Where's the way to that room?"

He smiled and then looked back and walked to the centre of the ground hall. He stopped exactly in the middle where the chair was placed, on which Arthur used to sit mostly while outside in the hall and sat some days back when they had a discussion. The chair was placed on a rug that covered the floor round. The rug was big and round and of light green colour. It had two big circles on it of lovely white and orange colours. He held the chair, placed it on the floor and said as he remembered something, "They said Arthur knew about it. I have no idea why Sir Arthur never discussed it with us, but they said he knew about it long before."

Caller started walking toward him and said something that she had never thought of in her dream that she would say. She confessed her hate for him, "Why is he doing it? I doubted him from the moment he talked badly to me. He doesn't seem like someone really keen to help us. He acts so mean and cheap sometimes. This cheap deed, hasn't he proven himself?"

Caller was acting so differently and none of them was able to digest what she said. There was a moment of silence and all of them standing there stared at her with blank faces of reactions and emotions. Arthur was a well-respected man among so many people, and he was even the main face of many good deeds and innovative works. Although his body was becoming so much weaker with age, his mind was exploding with something new every day, and staying in that caged building for a long time now, he was more of a depressed and introverted person. Arthur had been living in that building for the last three months. The situation three months before was not the same. However, people had started using this building as their shelter since most things were destroyed in earthquakes and the air too was a big reason. It was so quick. In half a year, the whole Earth was crushed down. Air, water, big buildings and even the soil were as if turned into ash. And now the entire Earth had rotted. The last thing that was keeping this building alive was a few plants inside the building. The plants inside the building were not more than one hundred, and these were not enough to fight against the whole Earth. Everything was decaying at a faster rate now. Now the building too had started craving for death, its bricks groaned as if in pain.

Bella waited for a moment for someone to break the long silence and raise their voice but no one really said anything, only Neviah said in a very polite way, holding her hands, "I don't think there's anything like that, he must have not told for the good reasons."
But Bella was not satisfied with his response. She walked to her, bumped straight into the back of her, held her hand and turned her one hundred eighty degrees. Bella looked into her eyes and said coldly, "What nonsense you think you're talking, huh?" She softened her voice as she talked about Arthur and said, "I agree that he hid this from us, but I'm sure he decided to do that for the right reasons." Bella's anger grew slowly again and said sharply, "You never talk like that about him, don't you ever talk about him or I swear you won't be able to talk! Did I make myself clear?"

"What the hell," said she and made a face.
Bella looked at her unbelievingly, her eyes hardened, and she absolutely had no idea what to say next. She looked at Neviah, "What's wrong with her?" then at her, "What is wrong with you?" and she turned back to Neviah and said, "Hell I'll show her. Get her out of my sight."

Neviah finally removed the rug quickly and opened the concealed trapdoor, revealing the entrance to the hidden underground room. He first looked at Cassandra and Caller but then he called out to that big man with a cut on his neck and told him to lead people into the underground room. There was a long spiral ladder in there that went down to the floor of the room. The time was short and they had to do everything fast. The big man looked at Bella and gave a little kind smile, but Bella was too busy thinking and had certain complex emotions going on in her mind. The man stepped on the stairs and went down slowly followed by Caller and Cassandra. And slowly everyone went one by one while Neviah stood there and looked at Bella apologetically.

"I'm sorry for being a little rude to you. I didn't mean to do that. I was so lost in the screen, being in a conversation with those people on the spaceship," said Neviah respectfully.

Bella smiled politely and said, "I didn't even think that you were being rude to me until you said it just now."

They both smiled at each other. Bella then suddenly gave a look of hurry on her face and said in a rush, "Quick, Neviah! We got to hurry."

She looked back at the door of Arthur's room and said, "Can you bring my children out of the room? They're in that room," she pointed to that room. Neviah nodded his head and walked at a fast pace toward the room. Bella thought for a second and then called out to him and said, "Or maybe I can go and bring them."

"No! No ma'am, you stay here and knock on Sir Arthur's door. He might not open, I'm afraid," said he.

Bella agreed and ran to Arthur's room. She knocked but no answer. She knocked again and kept knocking, hoping he'd open. After a few more tries, she had lost a little hope. While she was standing there, she felt a sense of déjà vu. She remembered the day when she was standing outside of the building with her children, waiting for someone to open the door. But this time it was only Arthur in the room alone, and only he could open the door. She looked around her and no one was really there. By then almost everyone was gone, and only Arthur, Neviah, herself, and her children were left. Bella tried once more and this time she knocked on the door hard and pushed the door with all her energy. Her heartbeat fastened and her ears felt warm. She waited for a moment in the hope that finally he'd open it. And finally, Arthur opened the door.

Bella looked at Arthur, who was unrecognisable. His eyes were deeper than the ocean on his face, and a black, dark shadow lingered under his eyes. His face was as if shrunk. Wrinkles were suddenly all over his face, making him look older and weaker than the age itself makes one look. But he smiled. He smiled when he saw Rachel. But his eyes talked more than his smile, and his eyes spoke of sadness and lostness. Bella was illiterate with the words then and couldn't find any word to utter, but only the tears were on shore, and some were about to fall. Arthur walked a little back. "Come in," he said with a tone of invitation.

Bella walked in and saw one yellow wall in the corner. It caught Bella's eyes, and confused she was because she had never seen something like that before. She looked closely, and it was mould. It was seen from a distance too that it was mould, but it didn't look like one — not exactly the same as the usual mould that she had seen, but it was quite different. The mould looked so alive.

She turned to Arthur and said, "But... but, isn't the growth of mould on the wall strange?"

"Right, right, I know," he assured.

Bella smiled a little in relief when she heard him speaking fine and the same as before — energetic, as if time only cursed his body's appearance but not the soul and mind.

"I've very little idea how it is here, but this mould is not just a simple natural part of nature. If it were natural, then it would be normal — but it's not. It grew on this wall just in a few minutes, and it talked to me."

Bella froze and asked in a shattered voice, with so many questions in her mind, "Wh...aat?"

"Yes! It talked to me," answered Arthur.

Bella asked what came into her mind first, "It talked to you? It talked to you what?"

Arthur looked at the moulds on the wall and said, "I have no idea what it talked about. I didn't understand it. It was so weird. But whatever it was, it didn't feel good. There were so many negative vibes around it — I felt it."

"It must be true that this seemingly untrue is not untrue, since we know what happened to this Earth in the last three months is no less than a dream. And this mould is no exception," said Bella, and walked a little closer to the mould.

"Bella, no, stop! Do not make the mistake of touching it," warned Arthur.

"Have you touched it?" asked Bella, as if she was never about to touch it.

Arthur didn't answer and remained silent, with a feeling of regret on his face. Bella read it.

"So, you did touch it, and I do not doubt your curiosity with such things. You must have dug into it. I do not doubt you. Am I right?" asked Bella with an upset voice, working up a slow anger.

"Yes, you are right."

"Are these moulds the cause of your current condition? Does time fly around these moulds?" asked Bella, a little curiously.

"I believe it so far," said he, and looked down at the floor for a moment and said, "That's a problem with every curious mind. They like to play, knowing it will burn — and it burns, but still they like the fire."

Bella walked a little closer to Arthur and said, "But aren't these people heroes only to the world and no less than villains to their own families by giving sorrow and grief in the process of saving the whole world? Do you even care about us?"

"I'll answer your question later, Bella," said Arthur with a big smile on his face.

There was not a moment's break between when Arthur finished his words and Neviah stopped by the door. Neviah looked at Sir Arthur and gasped. He ran toward him and hugged him tightly. Arthur patted his back gently while releasing the hug. Neviah looked at Sir Arthur again and asked him kindly, "Are you okay, Sir?"

Arthur nodded and said, "Yeah, I'm all good."

"Where are the kids?" asked Bella.

"They are here," said Neviah, and looked back. The children appeared at the door and ran to Bella as they saw their mother. Bella hugged them tightly to her chest and kept them close to her heart for many a moment. Neviah was a little nervous and excited simultaneously and wanted all of them to get to a better and safer place — the underground room. And so, automatically, his movements hastened and looked uneasy in and out, and he said finally, "We got to go now." They all agreed. Arthur collected his few books that were on the table and a diary and some other needful things, and Neviah helped him with carrying the stuff. Neviah saw the wall that looked gross, but he didn't ask anything, only simply followed Arthur out of the room.

One strange thing that neither Bella nor Neviah noticed was that Arthur had never been revealed to where they were exactly going, through which way, and whether the spaceship had arrived. He knew about the underground room, but he didn't know that they were going into it and would find a spaceship — not the spaceship, but a tunnel to the spaceship. So the question was: how did he know about it? Arthur didn't ask any questions and simply followed

Neviah and Bella underground. He had no confused face, rather walked determined and confident out of the room and to the underground.

When they reached, they found the big man — the one with a cut on his neck — there, waiting for them. The room was quite big. Bella was never pleased to see that guy. She always remembered the horrific death of a small, innocent girl. She looked at him and asked in a bitter voice, "What are you doing here?" He didn't answer, and before he could say something, Neviah spoke.

"He said that he wants to be available for help. He regrets his deed in the past and wants to repay by helping or to fight if any danger comes."

"That is a positive way to start," said Bella finally, with satisfaction.

Bella's eyes fell upon the room, noting its vast emptiness cast in black-and-white hues. Positioned on the left-side wall, at its surface, was the round entrance to the tunnel. Before the tunnel's entrance lay some black soil, hinting at recent activity. The tunnel resembled a cylinder in shape, its dimensions suited for human passage with ample width and height. On the face of the tunnel, five sharp, folded blades were visible, suggesting their use in excavating the wall to create the entrance. The height of the tunnel was just as good as one man could walk through very easily, and just a good width — the surface of it was not a round one, but flat to walk easily through it to the spaceship. It was quite dark in the tunnel, but after a short long walk, they passed beyond the darkness and entered the spaceship.

CHAPTER SEVEN

THE RED PLANET (MARS)

The first thing that was seen and seen everywhere was small and big glass domes. There were robotic harvesters that methodically tended to nutrient-rich crops, ensuring a steady supply of food for the colonists. It included bases that likely included all the essential infrastructure and resources needed to sustain a human presence there—things like living quarters, food and water production, energy generation, and life support systems. In the central plaza, citizens bundled in pressurised suits hurried between domes, their footsteps crunching against the fine soil. The air hummed with the sound of life—the whir of machinery, the chatter of voices over radio links. The idea was to create a stable, self-sufficient foothold that could support further exploration and development of the new frontier.

When they all reached Mars, they were kept in a different dome. Arthur was not there. He was under some treatment. Everyone was optimistic about Arthur's health except Bella. She was a little worried about him because she was aware of his situation. Around two hours had passed since Arthur was shifted to medical healthcare. One man entered the dome with a device in his hand. It was a photo of Bella on the device. The man searched for that face, and when he found Bella, he told her to come with him. As she was told, she followed him. She reached a room that smelled like a garden of fresh rose flowers. The air was fresh and chilly. Entering the room, she saw a beautiful caricature of vegetables captured in a funny way, dangling on the front wall near the entrance. Some vegetables were not even the ones that Bella had seen in her life. She moved her head slowly to her right side and saw Arthur resting on a bed. She walked quickly to his bed and exhaled in relaxation.

"I'm all good," he sounded tired.

"You will be good," she paused. "No worries."

"The doctors told me not to take long. They said they'll need to do some kind of surgery and many treatments."

"What surgery?" asked Bella, confused.

"They didn't talk openly about it. Just told me it's a surgery."

"It will be fine," smiled Bella.

"Yeah!"

"You wanted to say something," said Bella.

"Oh! Yes, yes. But I forgot," he paused and then continued, "It was something I wanted to tell you later."

"Something about the heroes," she said after a brief moment.

"Yes! You were saying... you said..." he looked to his left, not exactly remembering what it was.

Arthur finding it difficult to remember the very recent talk hit Bella hard emotionally. Her face withered. But anyway, she helped Arthur to continue his talk and said, "I said heroes give more remorse than the villains and that heroes don't really care about their own families."

Arthur smiled gently and continued to answer her, "We know we'll die someday. Someday it will be every one of us. When a hero dies, he dies proudly and happily with no remorse. Bella, some heroes are chosen, and so when they do something, they do it in the favour of humanity. Isn't it great to be chosen for great deeds? We heroes feel proud to be chosen for some work. Definitely, it's never easy for the hero to lead a personally tragic life for others' good, and neither has it ever been easy for the hero's family."

"But isn't it sometimes too early for a hero's death?" she asked.

"It's never too late, and it's never too early. It's just the right time," he answered.

The same man who took Bella there knocked on the door first and then entered the room. He gently asked Bella to leave the room and said that it was time for Arthur to rest. She nodded and left the room. She was transferred to that same dome near her children. Neviah was waiting for her, and when she appeared, he went to her with a face full of many confusions.

"Can I ask you something?" asked Neviah.

"Go ahead," said Bella.

"What was on that wall in Sir Arthur's room?" he asked with deep interest.

"It was fungi. It was so different from a usual one."

"Yeah, it looked different," he said with a little satisfaction.

"Anything else?" she asked tiredly.

"I was confused, and still I am," he paused. "Why didn't Sir Arthur tell us about the underground room?"

"It's an easy one to think about. Why don't you break down the question and ask yourself, why would he? Even if he had made up his mind, he must have changed it after the death of the small girl just because of our negligence."

Neviah spoke his fear to ask and questioned her, "Then why didn't Sir Arthur question us about anything on the whole way to the spaceship? He never knew the spaceship had arrived and that the underground tunnel was the way to the spaceship."

Bella said thoughtfully, "I believe the mould was the reason. He told me that the mould talks to him, but he never understood it. It must be that Arthur, somewhere in his brain, knew all about what was going on outside. It was the mould that was updating him."

"That fungus on the wall?"

"Yes!"

"How is that possible?" he cried in astonishment.

Bella looked tired and shattered with many emotions in her heart. She walked past Neviah without saying anything and comforted herself around her kids. Some days passed. The prophecy of aliens was wrong. But the Earth looked worse now from the outside, and whatever was left to humans was Mars.

It was the fourth night of Bella on Mars. It was quiet and peaceful. The stars were much brighter and looked bigger. It was then that people understood the importance of their home planet. Although Mars produced enough to sate people's hunger, it was never the same to people as Earth. The joy was always there—to be able to colonise Mars—but there always remained the remorse.

That same night, at midnight, doctors woefully declared the death of Arthur. When Bella heard about it, she was already confused by her emotions. She wasn't sure if it was new to her or if she had known before that it would happen.

Bella remained lying on the floor with her children, looking at the sky. They enjoyed looking at stars after a long time together and smiled, looking at the stars.

75

About The Author

Author

Mona is a content and creative writer. She began her writing journey after taking a year off following high school, uncertain of the path ahead. During that time, she developed a deep love for reading, which inspired her to start crafting stories of her own. Since then, she has written fiction across various genres, including horror, historical fiction, fantasy, and thriller.
This story is one she's excited to share.

Official Website: moanaofficial.com

www.ingramcontent.com/pod-product-compliance
Lightning Source LLC
Chambersburg PA
CBHW031758150726
47989CB00006B/2777